Anna FROM THE North Pole

Welcome to the North Pole!
Have you been here before?
I'll tell you all about it
and take you on a tour.

There aren't many people and there is much work to be done. I've learned many different skills; it keeps things very fun.

It's frosty all the time here,
covered in icicles and snow,
but I learned to farm the land
and plant vegetables that grow.

SPINACH

CABBAGE

I am a baker and a chef, making recipes to try. Bread, soup and stew; cookies, cakes and pie.

I am a doctor and a vet,
tending to the sick.
From the reindeer to the elves,
and even old Saint Nick.

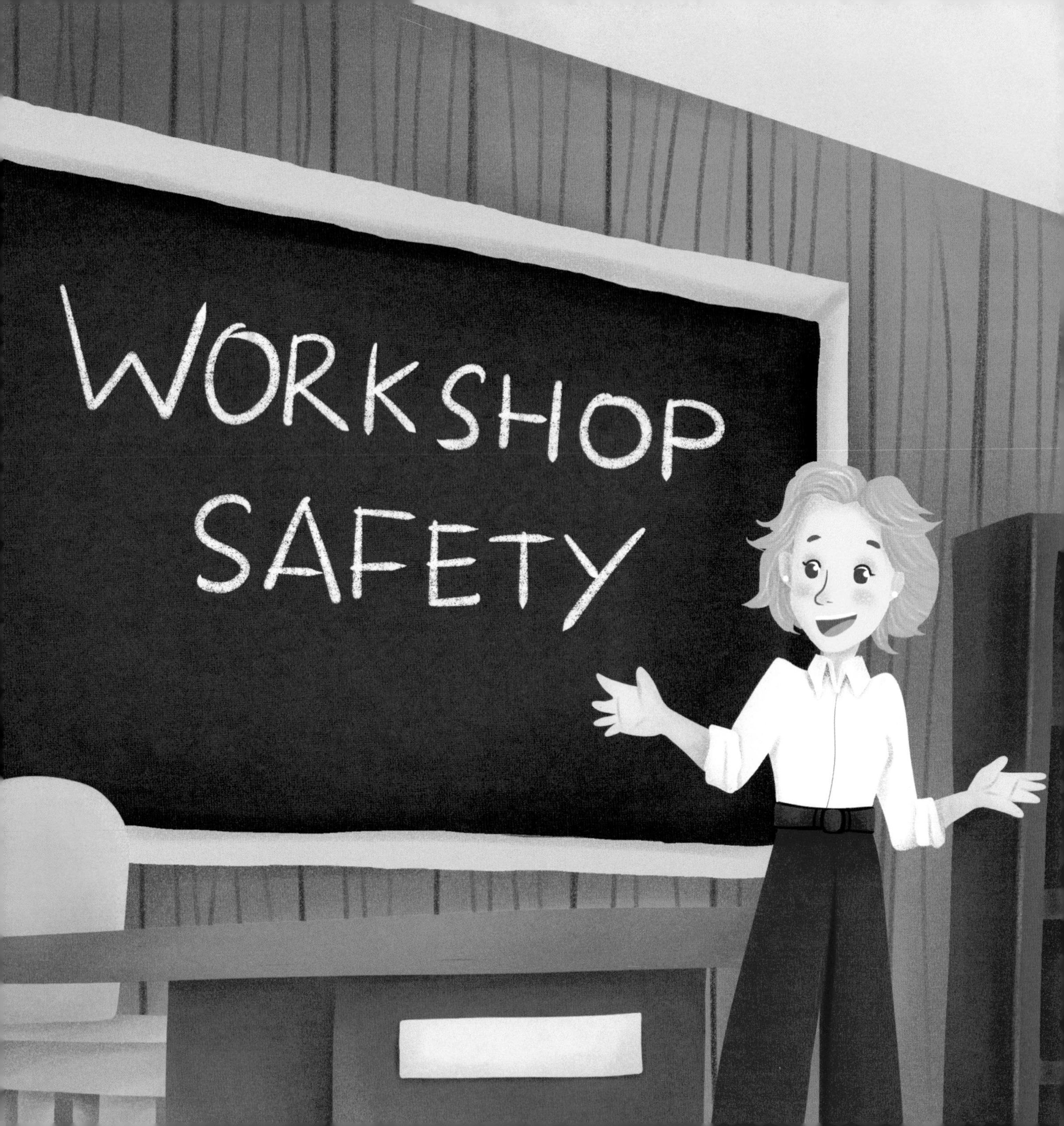
WORKSHOP
SAFETY

I am a teacher and a trainer,
sharing my skills with everyone I can.
And I keep learning too, there is
always something new to understand!

I design and sew all the clothes that keep us warm. Wooly sweaters and cozy coats that keep us safe in any storm.

I can build and fix things; houses – I've built ten!
I fixed the sleigh just last week, so it can fly again.

I am in charge of the post
sent from across the world.
Sorting every single letter
to answer every boy and girl.

I speak many languages so I
can read each letter.
Practicing every day,
always working to get better.

SPANISH

PORTUGUESE

I am so many different things,
adding new skills each day.
Toy designer, workshop manager,
and I can fix the sleigh.

Clothing designer and tailor,
I keep us warm in style.
When it comes to learning,
I always go the extra mile!
Farmer, baker and a chef;
a trainer and I teach.
Doctor, vet and postmaster,
nothing is out of reach.

Now you've seen the North Pole
and all the work I do.
My favorite jobs will always be
the ones I do for you.

I almost forgot to tell you
exactly who I am.
If you haven't guessed already,
now you probably can.

My husband is quite famous,
you know him as Santa.
Many call me Mrs. Claus,
but you can call me Anna.

Come and visit anytime,
there's so much here to do.
And when you come back next time,
I can teach you something new.

Anna FROM THE North Pole

by KRISTIN WILSON

illustrated by REZDEWI STUDIO

edited by ELIZABETH GEERLING